A Hero Named

Evander

A Hero Named Evander

Written and Illustrated

By

Brent Kevern

Printed in the United States of America
First Edition
The main body of text of this book is set in 12-point Helvetica.
ISBN 1-4486-4004-0

For Jared and Alaina ...

.... my heros and inspiration.

A special thanks to my editors, Sharon Coleman-Bock and Jennifer Dykes. Your hard work is greatly appreciated!

Table of Contents

Chapter 1

In the town of Craw Bucket, Missouri lived an athletically minded young boy named Evander. Evander had lived in Craw Bucket his entire life. This was rather unusual, as most people with even half of a working nostril had moved out of Craw Bucket many years ago to avoid the horrible smell that drifted down onto the town each day.

At one time, Craw Bucket had been a fun and friendly place to live. The people were pleasant and the town was alive with excitement, mostly centered on the town's popular football team. In the middle of the town sat a glorious football stadium that folks would pack each Friday night in the fall in support of their championship winning "Craw Bucket Eagles".

But unfortunately, the records being set by the town's football team were soon less important to the townspeople than the records being set by the town's new record holder: the Brownpile Stockyards, home of the world's largest collection of cows.

The smell from the stockyards had grown so intense over the years that even the hardiest Craw Bucket families soon found it too much to take and had packed up and moved away. But Evander knew that his family history had many roots in the town of Craw Bucket and no way would they be leaving anytime soon.

The smell from the town really didn't matter to Evander. He had much bigger concerns on his mind. Rather than spending his days trying to hide inside to avoid the "latest releases" from the brown pile cows, Evander could often be found outside running around doing what he enjoyed the most, playing sports.

Evander loved sports. He loved them so much that at times he found himself staying up all night just thinking about sports. Baseball, basketball, football, badminton.... you name it and Evander loved it. He loved to read about sports, write about sports, play sports, and draw pictures of sports. He even had named both his pet dog and cat "Sport".

Growing up a sports-loving kid in a town like Craw Bucket was not easy. Nobody but Evander dared venture outside for very long, and certainly not long enough to play sports, as the smell was just too strong. And so, Evander had done his best to entertain himself by playing sports alone. Throughout the years, Evander had grown frustrated with this as playing sports by yourself just isn't as fun as playing them with someone else.

Evander knew he could play baseball by himself... but not for long. It got tiring chasing the ball down, especially if he got a big hit. He knew you could shoot baskets by yourself and pretend to play basketball games, but he had grown bored with that too.

Evander wanted to play on a team! Most of all, he wanted to play on a real football team. It was his dream! It was his passion.

Then one day while daydreaming at school, Evander came up with a plan. Rather than waiting around any more, Evander decided it was time he took action. During the middle of the morning lesson, Evander tore a piece of notebook paper out of his notebook and on it he wrote "Football Team Sign-up" in big bold letters. Then he wrote the numbers 1 through 50 down the side. He got up, walked out of the classroom, taped it on the outside of the schoolroom door, and then he went back to class.

"Evander, what did you just do?" asked his teacher, Mrs. Nedermeyer.

"I put a sign-up sheet on the wall for a football team," answered Evander.

"In the middle of class? But, you could have disturbed the other student!" said Mrs. Nedermeyer, a look of disdain on her face.

"Uh, he's asleep Mrs. Nedermeyer, and that's not another student. That's the janitor."

"I know that Evander. And you could have woken him up. You woke me up didn't you?"

"Yes, Mrs. Nedermeyer."

"Well, next time you leave the class for some crazy idea like a football sign-up sheet, please do so quietly".

And so Evander agreed and sat back down in his chair and waited anxiously for the end of the school day. He couldn't wait to see if anyone had signed up for his team.

Chapter 2

Now, it would be nice to be able to say that Evander waited patiently for the school bell to ring and then got up and ran out of the room to check his list; however this was Craw Bucket and in Craw Bucket there wasn't a lot of need for a school bell, as Evander was the only student. Rather than listening for the bell to ring, Evander would just wait for Mrs. Nedermeyer to fall into a deep sleep. Then he would wait for the sun to come through the window and shine on Mrs. Nedermeyer's forehead. Once it reached her forehead, Evander knew it was time to go home.

So, at sunny forehead o'clock, Evander stood, picked up his textbook -- the same textbook he'd had for the last five years -- and quickly exited the classroom. His heart was beating a mile a minute as he turned the corner to check the list. But, much to his despair, the list remained empty.

"Darn!" thought Evander. "How am I ever going to get to play sports if nobody will play sports with me? This town really does stink!"

Evander thought hard about his dilemma that day on the way home from school. He considered all of his options. Could he convince his parents to have another baby? That would give him someone to play with. But then that would take forever and what if the baby didn't like sports? Maybe he could build a robot? That sounded like fun except he had no idea how to build a robot. Perhaps he could get some of the remaining townspeople to play with him if he asked really nice. Hmmm… that sounded like the best plan, even if there were only a few neighbors to ask.

Given that he really didn't have anything else to do, Evander decided to give his plan a try. He walked past the stockyard, holding his nose the whole way and made it to Mr. Eners' grocery store. He walked inside and called out for Mr. Eners. "Mr. Eners? You there?" Eventually, Mr. Eners came walking out of the back room.

"Hello Evander. How can I help you today?" asked Mr. Eners.

"I was wondering if you might like to play football with me on my football team."

"You have a football team?"

"Yup, I do. Would you like to play?"

"Son," said Mr. Eners "you must have blown a sprocket in that little brain of yours. I'm 82 years old! I can't play football. Heck, I can hardly walk! Now how am I gonna play football? And besides, it stinks out there!"

"Well, I was thinking it would be..."

"Enough of the nonsense boy! I got work to do!" said Mr. Eners, leaving quickly before Evander had even a chance to reply.

Disappointed, Evander opened the door, re-plugged his nose, and left.

Evander wasn't inclined to give up just yet though. There must be someone who wouldn't mind playing football with him, even if the town did stink. And then it dawned on him. What about the Brownpile family? They ran the stockyards in town. Certainly they didn't mind the smell! Maybe one of them would play.

And so Evander picked up the pace and headed towards the stockyards. The closer he got, the smellier it became. Eventually, Evander had to cover his nose and mouth with his t-shirt just to help him tolerate the stench.

He made his way through the stockyards and over to the Brownpile home where he saw Mrs. Brownpile hanging her laundry out to dry. It occurred to Evander that perhaps the Brownpile laundry wasn't the most wonderful smelling laundry in the world.

"Hi Mrs. Brownpile!"

"Well, hello Evander! What brings you way out here to see us?" asked Mrs. Brownpile, continuing to hang holey socks and faded jeans while she talked.

"I was wondering if any of you would like to play football with me on my team?" asked Evander hopefully.

"Well, Evander, that's all very nice, but I just don't think we can. We're so busy these days. With us nearing 7000 cows, we're up to our hips in doo-doo all day long. We just don't have time for games!"

Evander knew that was true. In fact, he could see Mr. Brownpile literally standing hip-deep in the doo-doo just beyond the fence near the Brownpile home.

"Oh. Well. Yeah. OK. I see what you mean. Well, if you change your mind..." began Evander, but by this time, Mrs. Brownpile had turned her attention towards returning to her kitchen. So Evander went on his way, relieved to be away from the overwhelming stench of the Brownpile business.

Chapter 3

So, what was a boy to do? Nobody in Craw Bucket wanted to play football with Evander and Evander wanted to play football. Evander gave up on the prospect of finding teammates and instead got himself into his uniform, found his football, got onto his bike, and rode downtown to the football stadium.

The field was named Poostain Plaza, not after the famous stains left all over the streets of Craw Bucket by the ever growing heard of cattle, but rather as a memory of Silus Poostain, the founder of Craw Bucket. Apparently, Silus and family had wandered the country looking for a place to raise their overly smelly cattle and had settled on Craw Bucket as the best place to do just that. As such, the townspeople that migrated to the village had named their football stadium in his memory.

The field was still in pretty good shape with the exception of the sometimes-longish grass. Evander had taken it upon himself to maintain the field by mowing it as often as he could find the time. He also repainted the yard markers with the free paint he'd convinced Mr. Eners to give him. Mr. Eners, for his part, thought the boy had totally lost his marbles and was happy to give him the white paint to get him out of his store.

When Evander arrived at the field, he found it in its usual state, needing a little bit of work and totally empty. He decided to procrastinate the mowing for the day. Instead, he got off his bike, walked out onto the field with his ball, and proceeded to play his simulated-one-man-football-team game.

Evander made his way out to the 50-yard line. He dug deep into his uniform pants to find the little pocket he had sewn in. It was a special place to hold his lucky quarter for the coin flip. Finding the coin, he proceeded to place it delicately upon his thumb. Then, he stated for nobody in particular, "Evander, please call it in the air!" He flipped the coin up and shouted out "Heads!" and, as usual, the coin came down "tails".

"Ah man!" exclaimed Evander, "I never get to receive!" He placed the coin back into his pocket and then stood motionless, attempting to feel which way the breeze was blowing. After careful consideration, Evander elected to defend the North goal. He didn't want "The Other

Evander" having an advantage of a wind–aided, late game field goal.

Evander took the ball, walked back to the 35-yard line and kicked his heel solidly into the ground, leaving a small divot in the grass. He continued to kick the same divot a few more times until he had enough of a hole to balance the ball in. Then, he placed the ball's tip into the hole, standing it straight on end. Evander backed up, raised his hand to signal his readiness, and ran full-steam towards the ball.

At just the right moment, Evander's foot made contact and the ball soared towards the opposite goal. At this point, Evander took off after the ball, running as fast as his feet could go. When he finally recovered the ball, he turned and assumed the role of "The Other Evander" and began running back up the field in pursuit of a touchdown. Unfortunately for The Other Evander, Evander was a fairly good tackler (or so Evander believed). But no matter what the truth, The Other Evander ran the ball back to the 25 yard line and then tripped in a previously dug field-goal-ball-holding hole, knocking The Other Evander down and nearly causing a fumble.

The Other Evander had Evander on the run for most of the first half and by the half-time break, was winning 21-7. Evander had completed a toss to himself with only one minute left on the game clock to successfully scoot around The Other Evander and get points on the board.

Evander knew that if he was going to win this game, he was going to have to outsmart The Other Evander, which wouldn't be easy since The Other Evander shared brains with Evander. Evander tried though. He sat on the bench at half time and tried to think of a new play while also whistling (which he thought would distract The Other Evander).

As the second half began, Evander looked like a boy possessed with the thought of winning. He did everything he could to outsmart The Other Evander. He dove when he should have spun. He threw passes to himself at moments when everyone would have expected him to run. The Other Evander held in there though and near the end of the 4th quarter, the score was tied, 28-28, with Evander having the ball on The Other Evander's 20 yard line. With just 3 seconds left, Evander called time-out so that he could get his kicking team (himself of course), out onto the field.

Evander backed up, took a big breath, and settled himself in. As the invisible center snapped the ball into position, Evander ran forward and made solid contact with the ball, sending it, with the aid of the wind, through the goal posts. Evander had done it!! He had beaten The Other Evander 31-28!

Evander was so excited. He couldn't remember the last time he had beaten The Other Evander! He ran over to the stands and did a "Lambeau Leap" into the empty bleachers. Since nobody was there to catch him, Evander came down hard on the bleacher pole knocking the wind clean out of him. He didn't care though. He'd done it! He'd finally won!

Evander didn't want the celebration to end and then, all of a sudden, it struck him how he could savor the victory. Looking up, he saw the scoreboard -- the same scoreboard he had stared at day in and day out dreaming that one day it would light up with a real score.

"Hmmm," thought Evander, "I'm gonna go for it!"

Evander climbed the bleachers and made his way toward the press box. When he got to the press box door he found the door locked, but not very securely. With a bump of his shoulder pads the door swung open. Much to Evander's delight, there sat the scoreboard control panel. Evander walked over to the panel and turned it on. The lights of the scoreboard flashed and immediately came to life. The score on the board showed 0-0. Evander clicked a few buttons and the score showed 31-28. He studied the control panel a bit more. For such a small town, the scoreboard sure seemed powerful. It even had the ability to label the team names on the board instead of it just always saying "Home" and "Visitors".

After a few minutes, Evander figured out a way to change the team names on the board to read "Evander" and "The Other Evander". It was nice to see his name up in lights, but it didn't seem quite right. Real teams would have real team names. Evander thought for a bit. After careful consideration he decided that from this point forward Evander would be named the "Eagles" and The Other Evander would be the "Giants". And so Evander changed the scoreboard one more time to read Eagles-31, Giants-28.

After successfully completing the scoreboard updates, Evander carefully closed the press box door, climbed down the bleachers, got back on his bike and headed home. As he neared the hill leading toward his home, Evander took one more look at the glowing scoreboard and smiled at the fact that Evander (now known as the Eagles) had finally won a game.

Chapter 4

The next morning Evander woke up and got ready for school. While putting on his socks, he remembered his triumphant victory the day before and smiled happily to himself.

After eating a big breakfast and loading up his backpack, Evander left his home and began his walk to school. In the distance he could see the scoreboard displaying the previous day's score. He made a mental note to return to the stadium after school and turn the scoreboard off.

The path to school took Evander downtown past Mr. Eners' grocery store and as he got closer, he noticed something highly unusual. Outside of Mr. Eners' store was a newspaper stand for The Daily Bucket, Craw Bucket's local newspaper. What was unusual was that there was actually a stack of newspapers on the stand! That never happened!

Long ago, the editor for The Daily Bucket, a nice man named Tom Chambers, had given up on trying to find something newsworthy to write about. He had ceased publishing papers and decided instead to spend his days fishing. The last time Evander could remember a newspaper being published was when Mr. Chambers had caught a trophy-sized bass and had used the paper to publish pictures of him kissing the bass full on the lips! Evander couldn't wait to read what had happened that would make Mr. Chambers come in off the lake long enough to publish a new edition of The Daily Bucket.

When Evander got close enough to the newspaper to make out the headlines, he could hardly believe his eyes. There in big type at the top of the front page were the words: "Eagles Beat Giants 31-28!!"

"What the heck?" thought Evander. "How in the world did Mr. Chambers know about my game?" Nobody was at the stadium during the entire time Evander played... he was sure of it! Mr. Chambers couldn't have seen him playing, could he?

Curious to find out what the article said, Evander dug into his pocket and pulled out fifty cents and gave it to Mr. Eners for the paper. Evander grabbed his copy, walked over, sat down on the curb and began to read:

"In a stunning upset, the Craw Bucket Eagles beat the Giants 31-28 last night in what was obviously the best home opener for the Eagles that this author can remember. The Craw Bucket Eagles narrowly edged the Giants to win the game. Everyone in attendance was thrilled to see this start to the season..."

Now, Evander was even more confused! How could Mr. Chambers have known about the game? Then, it dawned on him. The scoreboard! He'd left it on all night long. Mr. Chambers must have seen the scoreboard as he came back from the lake.

"Well," thought Evander, "I'll have to go talk to Mr. Chambers immediately after school and set the record straight!"

Evander folded up the paper, looked down at his watch, and determined that he was now late for school. He began to run. Just as he did so though, he looked over and saw Zeke from Zeke's Garage standing outside, holding his nose, but reading The Daily Bucket! And right next door at Bart-The-Barbers was good old Bart, also with The Daily Bucket in hand!!

Mrs. Lavender could be seen inside her flower store and she too, was reading the paper. "Did everyone in town know about the game?" panicked Evander. He really didn't have time to worry about it right now though as he had to get to school before the non-existent bell began to non-existently ring!

Evander burst through the front door of the school and ran into the classroom and couldn't believe his luck. Nobody was there! He had beaten the teacher to the classroom and the janitor hadn't begun his nap yet! How lucky for Evander! He was just sure he was going to get a tardy and ruin his perfect attendance record!

Evander overheard a conversation coming from the hallway. His teacher, Mrs. Nedermeyer, was talking very excitedly with someone about something! The door to the classroom swung open and Mrs. Nedermeyer walked in with the janitor following closely behind. Both had huge smiles on their faces.

"Oh, I'm sorry Evander! We're running a little late today. But, certainly you can understand. After all, the Eagles beat the Giants last night! Everyone is talking about it.

Can you believe it? What a great way to start the season!"

The only thought that Evander could think was "Oh… my…. gosh…"

Chapter 5

The class day started soon and it was not anything like a usual day. Normally, Mrs. Nedermeyer would ask Evander to open his book to page 132, -- yes it was always page 132 -- and work on the even-numbered problems. Evander had done the even-numbered problems so many times that he memorized the answers long ago. By habit, Evander opened his book to page 132, but Mrs. Nedermeyer didn't seem to care. Rather, she was sitting in one of the student desks (there were only three), talking endlessly to the janitor about the game!

"I'm so excited!! I'm thinking I'll need to get myself a new Eagles jersey," she declared.

"What the heck??" thought Evander, "Has she lost her mind? What does she mean by getting herself a new Eagles jersey?"

At that point, the janitor, who Evander had never heard utter a sound other than a snore, stood up and declared,

"That's a great idea! I wonder if we can get them after school at Eners' grocery store?"

Evander couldn't believe his ears. It was like the town had gone crazy! He decided that he needed to get the attention of Mr. Chambers so he could write another article explaining that the Eagles were just his made-up "Evanders" and nothing more -- and he figured he'd better do it quick! The town was going to go nuts unless he took action immediately!

"Mrs. Nedermeyer?" Evander called out.

"I'm thinking they could win again next week too! After all, our team is the best, don't you think?" blathered Mrs. Nedermeyer.

"Uh, Mrs. Nedermeyer?" Evander inquired again.

"Uh, well, uh, yes Evander? What do you want? Please be brief son. We've got a lot of talking to do today!"

"My stomach hurts. Can I go home please?" pleaded Evander.

"Sure, sure. Go right along now," said Mrs. Nedermeyer, turning her attention back to the janitor and the discussion of the game.

Evander got up, left the classroom, and began running back into town. He ran as hard as he could with hope he would find Mr. Chambers as soon as possible. Evander didn't bother stopping at the newspaper office. He knew Mr. Chambers wouldn't be there. It was a beautiful day and Mr. Chambers would assuredly be down at the lake fishing.

Evander arrived at the lake and ran out on the dock. Much to his surprise, the lake was empty and there was no sign of Mr. Chambers anywhere.

Defeated, Evander turned and headed back to town. When he got there, he saw Mr. Eners standing outside talking with Mr. Chambers!

"Oh, thank goodness!" sighed Evander.

"Mr. Chambers? Mr. Chambers?? We need to talk!" exclaimed Evander.

"Oh, hi there Evander! Good to see you again. Talk you say? Well, not right now, OK? I've got important newspaper business to attend to. Run along now..."

"But Mr. Chambers! It's about your article in the paper. You see, the Eagles are..." started Evander.

"I know... I know Evander. The Eagles are undefeated. Why do you think I'm out here? Mr. Eners was just telling me that he had ordered a whole collection of Eagles' jerseys as he is just sure there is going to be a rush to buy them, what with the team starting off so well this year. Now, please Evander let me get back to work."

And with that, Mr. Chambers turned his back on Evander and inquired of Mr. Eners, "So, you say you are ordering up a bunch of Eagles jerseys, eh? What sizes will they come in?"

Mr. Eners replied, "Oh, I suspect we'll have small, medium, large, and extra large available and maybe some kid's sizes too. After all, shouldn't everyone have a chance to show support for their team?"

Evander stood watching the conversation, his eyes bugging out of his head, his mouth hanging wide open. After a few more minutes, he had to leave. He just couldn't make sense out of what was happening. Eventually Evander made his way back home, walked into his bedroom, and plopped down on his bed. There next to his bed was his dog, Sport, currently gnawing on one of Evander's old tennis shoes.

"Sport, I think everyone in this town has lost their mind. They think the Eagles are a real team! I just made them up. I thought it would be fun to put the score on the scoreboard and... Oh no! I never turned off the board! Come on Sport! We gotta get down to the stadium and quick!"

Evander jumped out of bed and ran towards the door with Sport following right behind him. As soon as the door opened though, the dog screeched to a halt, took one whiff, sneezed, and ran back inside, leaving Evander to take the journey to the stadium by himself.

Evander rode like the wind to the stadium. When he got there, the scoreboard lights were still on showing the fictitious score of 31-28. Evander ran up to the press box, pushed opened the door, scurried over to the control panel and hit the "Off" switch. The lights on the scoreboard flickered and faded. Evander breathed a deep sigh of relief.

Chapter 6

After a good night's sleep, Evander felt much better. He was just sure all of the nonsense from the prior day would have ended and he'd be able to get back to page 132 and the even-numbered problems. Back to his normal, although sometimes boring, life! He got up, dressed, ate breakfast and headed out for school after patting Sport (the cat) on top of her head.

As Evander made his way towards town, he saw Mr. Eners standing outside his grocery store cleaning up. But, instead of the usual butcher's apron, Mr. Eners appeared to be wearing a bright, green, clean football jersey! When Evander got close enough, he could see in white print the word "Eagles" across the front of the jersey and the number 36 written underneath.

On the sidewalk, Mr. Eners was busily setting up tables and opening boxes upon boxes of jerseys. True to his word, there were small, medium, large, extra large, and kids sizes too!

Evander stopped, stared and shook his head, trying to clear his mind of what was truly not possible.

"Mr. Eners? What are you doing?" asked Evander

"Prepping the store for the big sale of course! Gonna sell me a ton of these Eagle jerseys today! Everybody who came in yesterday was asking for one. I'm thinking I just might be able to retire after this sale! Woo-hoo! Wouldn't that be a hoot?" declared Mr. Eners as he busily continued to prepare for his sale.

"But, Mr. Eners… there are no Eagles!!! This is crazy!"

"I know, Evander. I know. You are right. There is no picture of an eagle on the jersey. I had to take what I could get on such short notice. The t-shirt company didn't have time to print the picture of the bird, so I just went with these. I suspect they'll sell like hotcakes!"

"Oh for the love of Pete…" thought Evander, turning his back and walking away.

When he arrived at school, his teacher was in the room and the janitor was sleeping soundly in his chair, as usual, but there was one strange difference. Mrs. Nedermeyer was wearing an Eagles jersey!

"Mrs. Nedermeyer? Where did you get that jersey?" asked Evander. "I thought Mr. Eners just got them this morning?"

Mrs. Nedermeyer explained, "Well, Evander, if you must know, I stopped by Mr. Eners' store late last night looking for one of these jerseys. Mr. Eners had just arrived back from picking them up from the t-shirt shop. At first, he was reluctant to give me one, but he decided to do so if I would agree to accompany him to dinner on Saturday night. Of course, I immediately agreed. After all, I did want that jersey!!"

"Oh brother!" thought Evander.

"Now Evander, please sit down and let's get started. Open your book to page 132 and please work the even numbered problems," requested his teacher. Evander, relieved that some things had returned to normal, instantly began to reproduce the memorized answers on a clean sheet of paper.

When the clock struck "sunny-forehead o'clock," Evander packed his book up in his bag and left for the day. He should have expected what he saw next, but it still caught him off guard. Everyone in town was wearing an Eagles jersey! Even Mrs. Lavender could be seen wearing one inside of her flower store! Zeke, the mechanic, had found one big enough to somehow slide over his enormous belly. Evander figured that Mr. Eners must have ordered at least one triple-extra- large just for that purpose.

Evander had to admit the jerseys were pretty cool. And so he stopped by Mr. Eners' store himself. With the allowance money he had earned over the past few months he bought one in just the right size. It had a big number "18" displayed upon the chest. He slipped it over his head and went on home.

Evander was feeling so stressed out. Nobody in the town would listen to him and now everyone was thinking that the Eagles were a real team. When Evander felt stressed, normally, he would go outside and play sports. Today though, he wasn't just going to play. He needed to play hard. He needed to burn off all of the excess energy he had built up from worrying all day long. And, he needed to try out his brand-new jersey to see if it would fit over the top of his shoulder pads.

After dinner, Evander put on his gear and pulled his jersey over top of his head. With some help from his mom, he got it down over the top of his shoulder pads. The jersey fit like a charm. Evander had to admit he looked rather awesome with that big number "18" on his chest.

His mom, after attempting to straighten Evander's ever-messy hair, exclaimed, "My Evander! You look just like one of the real Eagles players in that jersey!"

Evander thought about trying to tell his mom the whole story, but decided against it, as he needed to get outside quick or explode with energy.

Evander rode his bike faster than ever on his way to the stadium. When he got there, he was surprised to see that the grass was cut short and the lines painted fresh! "Now how did that happen?" wondered Evander.

Evander ran out on the field and punted the football high in the air. Then, he caught up to it and punted it again. Back and forth, back and forth, he punted the ball. Soon, Evander was feeling a little better, a little tired, and a lot more relaxed.

Evander sat at the 50-yard line for a moment and thought about his last few days. Things had sure gone crazy in his town. People in Craw Bucket were known for their goofy side, but this was way beyond what Evander would have ever expected. "No matter," thought Evander, "they'll go back to just being weird soon enough. But right now, I need to play!"

And so Evander began his game. It wasn't even close this time. The Evanders, also known as the "Eagles" trounced The Other Evanders, today known as the "Rangers", 42-10. It would have been 42-3 had the Eagles not fallen for the late-game double reverse, but they had and so Evander had to settle for the 42-10 victory.

Feeling foolish for having worried so much about the crazy townspeople, Evander decided to have one more good laugh. He climbed his way to the press box and entered the final score: Eagles-42, Rangers-3. Giggling with his newfound ease, Evander walked home, again leaving the scoreboard ablaze for the entire town to see.

Chapter 7

Evander always enjoyed the weekends as it gave him not only time away from Mrs. Nedermeyer and school, but also he got to sleep in! He awoke at about 10:00 a.m. that morning and slowly shlunked his way into the kitchen, plopping down on the kitchen chair. His mom was busy making his favorite breakfast. She hardly noticed Evander had arrived in the room until the chair squeaked across the floor.

"Oh! Good morning, Evander! You startled me! Did you sleep well?" she asked.

"I sure did, Mom. I love the weekends, and especially Saturdays!" replied Evander.

"What will you be doing today, Evander?"

"Hmm, I don't know. Maybe watch some TV or play some video games. Not sure yet."

"Really?" his mom asked, looking curiously over her shoulder. "I'd have thought you'd have been downtown by now talking sports with the rest of the townspeople, what with the Eagles running their undefeated record up to 2 and 0 last night."

This revelation woke Evander right up and the groggy feeling he had was now a thing of the past. "Excuse me?"

"Well, Evander! I'm so surprised by you! I would have thought you'd have been all over the Eagles' score this morning, what with you being such a sports fan. Here…" she said, handing Evander a new edition of The Daily Bucket.

And there, in even bolder headlines than the day before, were the words "Eagles Trounce Giants 41-10!!" Evander noticed that the paper was a little bit thicker today than usual. He flipped through it and found an article on the game…. his game. There were also all kinds of interviews with the townspeople discussing the Eagles at length. Smack dab on the cover of the paper was a picture of Mr. Eners proudly displaying his empty boxes of Eagles jerseys.

"I can't believe this!" said Evander.

"Me neither!" said his mom, "Who'd have thought that the Eagles would be off to such a rip-roaring start?"

"Well, certainly not me!" said Evander.

"Now Evander, I know you are a huge sports nut and so I went down to the store last night and got you this," said his mom as she handed Evander a brand new bright green and white Eagles pennant.

"Mom, you shouldn't have. I..."

"You're welcome, Evander. Now, hurry along and go hang it in your bedroom!"

"Oh, OK. Thanks Mom," said Evander as he made his way back to his bedroom.

"Man, that seemed like a funny joke last night, leaving the score up on the board again. I can't believe this town!" exclaimed Evander. He took the newspaper with him as he went to his room.

Mr. Chambers had done a heck of a job writing up a game that he couldn't possibly have seen played. The article started off as follows:

> "The Craw Bucket Eagles continued their dominant season last night with an impressive win over the hapless Rangers. The game appeared tight for a while with many a punt seen hanging in the air, but eventually, the Craw Bucket Eagles turned their wings toward the sky and showed those Rangers a thing or two about playing football, placing a score of 42-10 into the record books..."

"Not again!" said Evander. "I have got to talk some sense into Mr. Chambers and I have to do it right now!"

Evander quickly pulled on his pants, slid into his new jersey, and left on his bike in pursuit of Mr. Chambers. He found him exactly where he had now grown used to seeing him -- right inside Mr. Eners' grocery store.

"Mr. Chambers, we really need to talk!" shouted Evander.

"Hi, Evander! I'll bet you are excited about the Eagles' victory. I'd love to interview you for the article. Maybe get a kid's perspective on how the Eagles are affecting you, perhaps motivating you to do better at school or work out harder in the gym…"

"Uh, well, no that's not what I wanted to talk to you about…I, uh…"

"So, have you been going to school lately?"

"Well, sure. But I…"

"Would you say that the Eagles have made this town a bit more interesting?"

"I would definitely say that."

"And do you think you speak for all of the kids at your school when you say you would like to be an Eagle someday?"

"I am an Eagle. In fact, I'm the only Eagle!" Evander tried to explain.

"Oh, that's so cute Evander. I know you probably do feel like the Eagles' biggest fan, as you are the biggest sports nut we have here in Craw Bucket. But I'm thinking this is everybody's team. Thanks for the interview! I gotta get out of here and get working on tomorrow's lead story. Perhaps you'll see your name in the paper tomorrow, Evander! Wouldn't that be swell?"

"Yeah, swell," Evander agreed halfheartedly, thinking that one day soon he'd definitely be seeing his name in the paper, but not for the reason Mr. Chambers had meant for him right now.

Evander thought for a minute and decided once again that he needed to try to get through to Mr. Chambers. He caught up with him in the back of the store and tugged on his coat sleeve.

"Mr. Chambers, can I ask you a quick question?"

"Sure Evander. But make it quick. I really am busy."

"Mr. Chambers, have you ever seen the Eagles play?" asked Evander.

"Well, of course not son. There's no way I could sit outside amidst all that cow smell! What do you think... I'm crazy? Of course, I can see the ball flying around the stadium from my office at night, and I can see the scoreboard, so it's almost like being there."

And with that said, Mr. Chambers walked to the front of the store and left.

Evander now understood at least where the stories were coming from. He should have caught on earlier that Mr. Chambers was not writing about what he had seen. That would have required him to leave his office (or the lake) and there was no way Mr. Chambers would do that voluntarily.

Just then, Mr. Chambers came back in the store and said, "Oh, one more thing Evander. What do you and your classmates think the Eagles' chances are against the Panthers next week?"

"The...P...P...P...Panthers?"

"Yeah, you know...The Martin City Panthers. You must have heard by now that Mayor O'Brian challenged the

Martin City Panthers to a game next week. It's in all of the papers!" Mr. Chambers said with a wink, holding up a copy of his own Daily Bucket. Right there, on the back page was the article: "Mayor extends invitation to Martin City Panthers to take on Craw Bucket Eagles next week!"

As everyone knew, the Martin City Panthers were the biggest, meanest, toughest school football team in all of Missouri. Evander had followed them very closely for years. The thought of playing against the Panthers made Evander dizzy. He whispered weakly to the overly excited Mr. Chambers, "I think I better sit down."

Chapter 8

That afternoon, Evander did something he hadn't done in a very long time. He climbed the rope in his backyard to the tree house he and his dad had built together when he was younger. Long ago, Evander had filled the tree house with some of his very favorite sports memorabilia. He remembered how when he was younger he'd climb the rope each day after school. He'd spend hours up top, reviewing his favorite football cards, going over the day's sports statistics, re-enacting his favorite plays. It had been a great place to sit and think. If there was anything Evander needed to do right now, it was sit and think!

And so he climbed and upon reaching the top, remembered why he hadn't been inside the tree house in a while. Evander had grown quite a bit since those days and the tree house now made for pretty cramped-quarters. After some wiggling around, Evander was able to get himself inside. Even though he was pinched in, the tree house still had that same calming-effect.

Evander found his football cards exactly where he had left them, inside a small drawer he had built into the side of the tree house. He pulled out the cards one by one, recalling each player's name and vital statistics.

He continued to flip cards until he arrived at his all-time favorite, Bruce Jones, the defensive tackle for the Missouri Bears, Missouri's very own professional football team. Bruce Jones was a huge man. He stood 6-feet, 6 inches tall and weighed 290 pounds. They said his hands were so big he could palm two basketballs with one hand.   Evander thought this was probably a bit of an exaggeration.

"What would Bruce Jones do in this situation?" Evander wondered. "Hmm. Well, he probably wouldn't have gotten himself into this situation in the first place!" Evander said, feeling sorry for himself.

After pondering his dilemma a little longer, Evander suddenly had an idea. "I know what he'd do! Bruce Jones would take on those Panthers and demolish them one by one!" Evander exclaimed, raising his fists in a mini-victory dance.

It was then that Evander decided to stop feeling sorry for himself and to instead focus on becoming just like Bruce

Jones. He would show those Panthers a thing or two on the football field. Why, all he had to do was work out until the big game. Surely by the time the Panthers took the field, Evander would be enormous and intimidating, just like Bruce Jones. And surely those Panthers would run away and hide once they saw how huge Evander had become.

So, Evander climbed out of the tree house and slid down the rope. He went into his basement and began to lift weights. He lifted and lifted and lifted until he just couldn't lift any more. Evander collapsed on the floor, panting, sweaty, and not one bit larger.

But that didn't stop Evander. As soon as he recovered, he lifted weights again and continued on into the night.

The next morning, a brisk but sunny Sunday, Evander climbed out of bed early and ran to the bathroom mirror to see what would certainly be his newfound piles of muscle. Much to Evander's disappointment, there were no new visible muscles. There were certainly sore muscles though! Evander attempted to lift his arms up to comb his hair and couldn't even come close to getting the comb into his hair. He was too sore!

"Oh, great!" thought Evander. "Now what am I going to do? I can't even move let alone play football and the Panthers will be here next week!"

Evander decided that even if he couldn't move, Bruce Jones would still get up and go play football. So Evander put on his uniform and went down to the stadium to practice. He practiced hard. At the end of his simulated game, he had won again, this time beating the Rams 16-12.

After the victory, Evander once again posted the score on the scoreboard. He knew the townspeople would be excited to see another victory. He wanted them to be happy again (at least one more time) before the Panthers came in and destroyed him.

And, Evander was right. The townspeople were ecstatic with the news of the latest victory. In fact, they had arranged to have a big banner that read "Home of the Eagles" erected over the top of downtown's Main Street. One storekeeper had even gone so far as to paint "3 – 0" in bright green paint on his shop's front window.

Everywhere you looked, there were people actually outside. They were wearing Eagles jerseys and talking excitedly. Everywhere you looked, Evander felt, you could see people that would one day be really mad at him for creating this scam.

But right now, Evander couldn't worry about that. He had to spend his time worrying about how not to die when the Panthers came to town and annihilated him on the football field!!

Evander continued to lift weights, run, and practice football with every free moment he had. He even slipped out of school early most days (at sun-on-the-ear o'clock) to get some extra time on the field. On one afternoon, he spent at least two hours trying to palm two basketballs at once. He thought he had it for a second, but then they both dropped. Yeah, he knew that the two basketballs he was working with were mini-balls, but still, it would have been awesome to be able to do two basketballs, even if they were tiny.

Before he knew it, the week had flown by and it was the night before the big game. Evander decided to go to bed early that night and try to get as much rest as he could.

He figured it might be his last night in his own bed, what with the Panthers probably putting him in the hospital the next day.

Surprisingly, Evander did sleep that night, although not well. For most of the night he dreamt about huge mountains chasing him around and falling on top of him. He wasn't exactly sure what that dream was about, but he knew he didn't like it all that much.

Chapter 9

Evander awoke with a start, recalling immediately that it was game day. The day he knew that would soon mean his demise. He dreaded getting out of bed.   But he knew Bruce Jones would do it and so he swung his legs over the side. He rocked his body forward and put both legs down, accidentally stepping on the back of his dog, Sport.

Sport looked up at Evander and stood, turned, and licked the boy's toes. Evander giggled at that. He was amazed at how such a simple gesture could help him relieve some of the worry he was feeling.

"Thanks, Sport!" Evander said as he patted his dog on the head. "You're a great pooch."

Evander got up, slipped on his slippers and walked to the kitchen where he found not only his mother, but also his father sitting around having breakfast.

"Ready for the big game today son?" asked his dad, a burly man who also was known to have loved sports in his day.

"Not really," proclaimed Evander.

"Hmm. That doesn't sound like you! I thought you'd be the Eagles biggest fan!" said his dad.

"I'm a fan, I guess. Just not as big of one as I had hoped to be by now."

"Well, keep rooting for them and we'll see what happens. My money's on the Eagles taking it to those Panthers today."

Evander thought about that for a minute and was really hoping his dad hadn't bet any "real" money on the "fake" Eagles. That's all the family needed! First, a destroyed son with probably football cleat marks run up and down his body AND no money to pay for the obviously needed surgery.

Evander ate a quick breakfast of a plain piece of toast (his stomach couldn't handle anything more) and then walked slowly on back to his bedroom. He had two more hours before game time and he needed to review his playbook at least once more.

After reading through his notes and deciding on his plays, Evander put on his uniform, climbed on his bike and rode off to meet his doom.

Evander got to the stadium about a half hour early. Much to his delight, nobody was sitting in the seats. The fall breeze had really stirred up the stench from the stockyards and Evander was not surprised that nobody was in attendance. He was also very happy to see that the Panthers had not yet arrived, meaning that he had time to work through a few of his key plays before they showed up and could see what he had planned.

After working through the plays and stopping to get a drink of water, Evander was puzzled to see that the Panthers had still not yet arrived. "What the heck is going on?" he wondered. "Do I have the wrong time or day?" Evander picked up his gym bag and pulled out his old copy of The Daily Bucket that had announced the game. He looked closely at the article and confirmed what he had believed. The mayor had challenged the Panthers to a game at 2:00 p.m. on this very day.

"Where could they be?" Evander wondered.

He decided to take a breather and sat down on the bench on his side of the field. He sat for about 15 minutes and then decided that certainly something must have happened.

And then it dawned on him! Maybe the Panthers knew about Craw Bucket. Maybe they knew how bad it stank here (especially inside of Poostain Plaza). Maybe, he had gotten extremely lucky and the Panthers weren't going to show up! Could he really have escaped his death so easily?

Evander waited another 15 minutes. He then got up, threw his helmet high in the air, and danced and cheered. He ran up to the press box and recorded the score he had devised to show the forfeit to his fellow townspeople: Eagles 7 – Panthers 0.

Evander laughed and giggled. He ran to his bike, amazed at how he had escaped sudden death at the hands of the Panthers. He got on his ride and decided to head over and buy himself a soda at Mr. Eners' store.

He wasn't surprised to see that just inside of Mr. Eners' store was a large crowd of townspeople! They were all dancing and cheering and wearing their jerseys and pointing to the big scoreboard over at Poostain Plaza.

"We won! We WON! The Eagles are 4 and 0!" yelled Mr. Eners himself. Mr. Chambers was dancing the jig in the background, while trying to write down every great quote he heard. Mrs. Lavender had Eagle-fever and brought over numerous green and white flowering plants to help commemorate the day and to make Mr. Eners' store look even more "Eagle-ish" as she described it.

"Evander? Did you go to the game today?" asked Mr. Chambers, now getting himself back in control. "I saw you come out of the stadium all dressed in your uniform. How did our boys look? Are they bigger than those Panther thugs?"

"Well, the Eagles were definitely bigger than the Panthers today!" answered Evander truthfully.

"Awesome. Just awesome!" proclaimed Mr. Chambers, "Can I quote you on that?"

"Sure," said Evander.

Just then, Evander heard the unmistakable blaring of the horn of Mayor O'Brian's personal, chauffeur-driven limousine. The dark limo came screeching around the corner and skidded to a stop. The mayor's chauffeur, James, hopped out of the car, held his nose, and opened the backdoor for the mayor's arrival.

Now Mayor O'Brian was a special man, uniquely qualified to run the town of Craw Bucket. When Mayor O'Brian was younger, he had worked in the stockyards right alongside the rest of his brothers and sisters, trying to help his family make an extra buck. Unfortunately, while shoveling a nice, heaping pile of poo, the mayor failed to look where we has scooping. He was unceremoniously kicked square in the face by one angry heifer. The point of impact -- cattle hoof to mayor face -- was precisely and squarely upon the mayor's snout, cutting his nose completely off of his face!

In an odd twist, the mayor was no longer susceptible to being overwhelmed by the stench of the town. Rather, he could stand outside for hours and not be bothered at all. Because of this "gift," he had found that he was the

only one who could campaign for the job of mayor. He
was the only one who could stand the smell long enough
to deliver a speech outdoors.

So, year after year, the mayor won re-election, even
though most of the townspeople didn't think he actually
did all that much.

The mayor got out of the car, and with a pompous walk,
sauntered into the grocery store through the front door.
The townspeople politely clapped their hands and made
way for the mayor so that he might take a position on top
of one of the milk crates to deliver what was undoubtedly
yet another boring and seemingly endless speech.

"Thank you! Thank you! People of Craw Bucket, I thank
you!" began the mayor.

"Today, we have seen the defeat of one of our udder
enemies…" (The mayor was like that, always inserting
cow phrases into every sentence that he could, kind of as
his way of bragging about this town). "They mooooved
backwards in defeat as we milked them for all they were
worth."

Most of the townspeople groaned at this point.

"I was on hand for this game and I must say, our Eagles looked very brave out on that field! In fact, there was one point where the Panthers must have hit one of our players very hard as his helmet was seen flying high into the air!" The crowd "ooh-ed" and "awed" as he proclaimed his visions.

"Uh-oh," murmured Evander. "Had the mayor seen the game?" If so, he was in for BIG trouble now.

"But our Eagles came throoooooough, ladies and gentleman. Not one of them cow-ered out of the way. Not one of them would be steered away from victory!"

"As such, and in proud recognition of this most glorious event, I hereby declare tomorrow "Eagle Day" in Craw Bucket! And to commemorate this important day, I declare that beginning at 10:00 tomorrow morning, a parade will be held down Main Street. The Eagles' team is invited to ride in the parade to hear our screams of joy for what they've accomplished!"

"Hooray! Hooray for the Eagles!" shouted the townspeople. All, of course, except for Evander.

"A parade? Oh no!" groaned Evander. How in the heck was he going to pull off a parade? What should he do? What would Bruce Jones do???

Chapter 10

As the crowd moved around, Evander found himself a place to sit and dropped quietly onto the ground. He was definitely toast now. The townspeople would see him riding by himself in the parade and they would know that the jig was up. He'd be made a laughingstock.

Instead of having fun and playing football, Evander figured he had pretty much ruined his life. All he wanted to do was play sports. All he wanted to do was compete with some friends, to tackle a non-invisible opponent, to maybe suit up in a real uniform with real referees with their own coin to flip. But now look at the mess he was in.

It was hopeless, thought Evander. Absolutely hopeless.

Evander's head slumped low beneath his shoulders, so low that he almost didn't see the shiny black shoes approaching from his left.

"Evander?" said a voice from above.

"Not now. I'm thinking," said Evander.

"Evander, my boy. That's no way to talk to your mayor! Now looky up here I say! Look now!" said the mayor, his big, round belly looming large over the top of Evander's head.

"Oh, uh, I'm sorry your honor. I didn't realize it was you. I'm really sorry."

"It's OK, boy. It's OK. Mind if I have a seat?"

"Uh, sure your honor," Evander said, sliding to the side. He watched the rotund mayor drop first slowly to his knees and then ever so clumsily over onto his backside.

"Evander, my boy, that was quite a game, don't you think?"

"Yes sir. I suppose."

"Well, I think it was. After all, you've personally never looked better out on that field."

Uh-oh! The mayor had seen the game. Oh no! Evander's goose was cooked. He was going to jail. He was going to be locked up by the mayor himself and the key would be thrown away for 1000 years.

"I don't know what you are talking about sir," pretended Evander.

"Oh, sure you do boy! Come on now. You can't kid a kidder. I saw you out on that field today. I know the Panthers didn't show up. In fact, I know why!"

"You do?"

"You bet I do. This town stinks! There's no way those pretty-boys are going to come down here and get their noses all clogged up with cow-doodie. No way!"

"Then why did you invite them, your honor?"

"Because, boy! Look at what has happened to this town! Why, people are excited! People are celebrating! People have rallied around the Eagles. This town has come alive again! And, Evander, I might add, that it is all because of you!"

"Me sir?" said Evander with deep surprise.

"Why of course, you!" explained the mayor. "It was you that came up with the football team. It was you that played the games. It was you and your undying love of sports that brought great joy to this town. You, Evander, are a hero!"

"But sir, tomorrow, the parade??"

"That's right, Evander. Tomorrow, there's going to be a parade. And the entire Eagles team is going to be there!"

"But sir, I am the entire Eagles team."

"Indeed you are! And tomorrow, we will celebrate. We will celebrate you and your gift to our community!"

Evander didn't know what to say.

Chapter 11

The next day, Evander arose as usual, ate his breakfast as usual, and walked downtown. He expected to find a mob of people waiting to hang him from the town water tower while they threw water balloons at him.

But that's not at all what Evander saw. Rather, there in front of him was a street lined with people. Not people inside their stores, but people standing outside, on both sides of the street! Nobody was holding their nose. Everybody was too busy clapping.

As Evander walked closer, he saw the mayor coming to greet him. The mayor grabbed Evander's hand, and shook it firmly. Then, in one elegant swooping-move, the mayor picked the boy up. He placed him directly on his shoulders and walked right down the Center of Main Street

As Evander rode, he waved at all of the cheering townspeople. There were people outside that he hadn't seen in years -- people young, old, from near and far, even people that had moved away from Craw Bucket years before. All of them had come out to participate in the parade celebrating Evander!

At the end of the parade there stood a large podium. After the mayor finished his walk, he took Evander up on the podium and held his hands up high. The townspeople cheered so loud Evander's ears began to ring.

"Evander, you are our hero! You have re-awakened this town. You have helped us make new friends and to renew old acquaintances. You have given us a new spirit. You have helped us see what we have been missing all of these years. You, Evander, are our hero! And to you, we give the key to our city!"

With this, the mayor handed over a large gold colored key to Evander, which Evander took and held closely to his chest.

"Evander, thank you! Thank you from the bottom of our toes to the smelliest part of our nose! You, Evander, are our very favorite Eagle."

Evander stood in front of the crowd, shaking, a tear coming to his eye. This time though, the tear wasn't brought on by the overwhelming smell of the stockyards, but by the overwhelming emotions Evander was now feeling.

"Evander, as a reward for your achievements, I, Mayor O'Brian, declare that from this point forward, Craw Bucket will be known as the town of the undefeated Craw Bucket Eagles. Further, I am pleased to announce that after last night's win, we have received the signatures of 25 boys from around the county who are interested in joining up to play on the Eagles' team next season. We need just one favor from you, Evander... would you please do this town the honor of being the captain of the team?"

With a smile bigger than any he had ever smiled, Evander nodded yes and the townspeople cheered with great joy.

That next year, the Craw Bucket Eagles did indeed field a team with Evander as their proud captain. And, as would become a tradition for years to come, the Craw Bucket Eagles were undefeated at their home stadium; most recently renamed Craw Bucket Coliseum – Home of the Evander Eagles.

About the Author

Brent Kevern was always telling stories. His kids and their friends couldn't wait to hear the latest addition to his chronicles that began as simple bedtime tales. Brent decided to share his stories with even more families by publishing his first book, *A Hero Named Evander.*

Brent enjoys spending time with his children, writing stories, creating technology, and studying Science. He works at a Children's Hospital in Kansas City, Missouri looking for ways to make sick kids well. In his spare time, Brent takes pleasure in coaching, watching, or playing his favorite sport...baseball.

Brent currently lives in Olathe, Kansas with his two children.

Made in the USA
Lexington, KY
05 March 2010